The Pups Save Christmas!

Adapted from the teleplay by Ursula Ziegler Sullivan

Illustrated by Harry Moore

🌸 A GOLDEN BOOK • NEW YORK

© 2015 Spin Master PAW Productions Inc. All rights reserved. Published in the United States by Golden Books,
an imprint of Random House Children's Books, a division of Penguin Random House LLC, 1745 Broadway, New
York, NY 10019, and in Canada by Random House of Canada, a division of Penguin Random House Ltd., Toronto.
Golden Books, A Golden Book, A Big Golden Book, the G colophon, and the distinctive gold spine are registered
trademarks of Penguin Random House LLC. PAW Patrol and all related titles, logos, and characters are trademarks
of Spin Master Ltd. Nickelodeon and all related titles and logos are trademarks of Viacom International Inc.
randomhousekids.com
ISBN 978-0-553-52391-1
Printed in the United States of America
10 9 8 7

It was the day before Christmas. The PAW Patrol pups were excited to decorate the big pine tree outside the Lookout.

"These old tennis balls will make great decorations," Chase said.

He pushed a lever on a small catapult that Rocky had made and launched a green ball up onto a branch.

"I love Christmas," Zuma said with a sigh. "I can't wait for Santa to get here."

"I've got the popcorn!" Ryder announced as he walked out to the tree.

Rubble ran alongside him. "Hooray! A Christmas Eve snack!"

"This isn't for eating," Ryder said. "It's for hanging on the tree."

"Okay," Rubble replied. "My eyes will like popcorn on the tree, but my tummy would rather eat it."

Everyone worked together. Ryder strung his popcorn along the branches, and Rocky hung lights. Marshall parked his fire truck next to the tree and raised the ladder so he could put ornaments on the highest branches.

When the pups were done, the tree was beautiful, but they agreed that something was missing.

"A star!" Skye exclaimed. "We need to put the star on top. I'll do it!" Wings popped out of her Pup Pack as she grabbed a star from the ornament box.

Skye zoomed to the top of the tree and placed
the star there. All the pups cheered.
"Now we know Santa will find us!" Skye declared.

Later that night, Ryder watched his Santa Tracker on the Lookout's viewing screen. It showed a big blizzard on the horizon—and Santa was flying right into it!

"What's Santa going to do?" Zuma asked.

"Don't worry," Ryder said reassuringly. "If anyone can fly through a bad winter storm, it's Santa."
But at that very moment, Santa was having trouble.

The storm rocked Santa's sleigh back and forth.
Bags of presents fell out, and a big golden star
slid off the front.

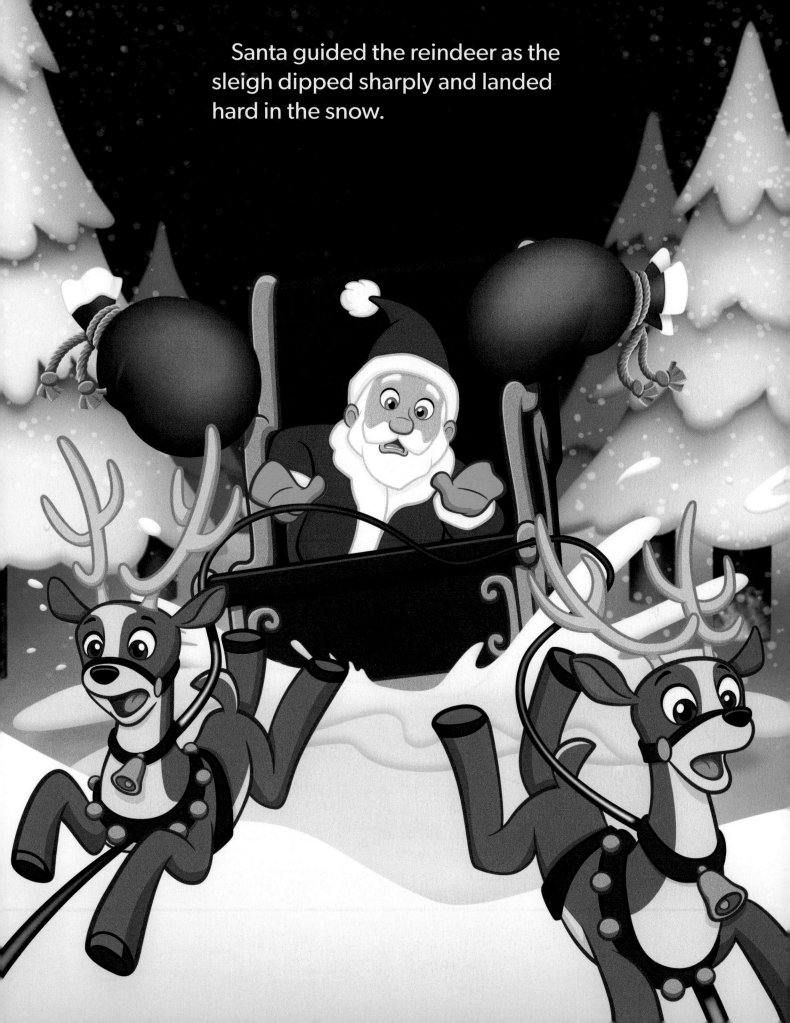

Santa guided the reindeer as the sleigh dipped sharply and landed hard in the snow.

Back at the Lookout, Ryder received a call on his
PupPad. It was Santa Claus!
  "My sleigh crashed, and I lost a load of gifts," he
said. "My reindeer are lost now, too, and worst of all,
my Magic Christmas Star is gone. That's what gives
my sleigh and reindeer the power to fly! Without it, I'll
never finish delivering my gifts!

"I need you and the PAW Patrol to help save Christmas," Santa said.

Ryder gasped. "Save Christmas? Us?"
"I thought there was no job too big and no pup too small," Santa said with a smile.
Ryder nodded. "You're right, Santa. We'll do everything we can to help!"

Ryder told the pups about Santa's problems. "Rubble, I need your shovel to dig the sleigh out of the snow."

"Rubble on the double!" Rubble shouted.

Ryder looked at Rocky. "I need your forklift to help raise Santa's sleigh out of the snow, and some recycled parts to fix it."

"Don't lose it—reuse it!" said Rocky.

Ryder continued. "Skye, Zuma, and Marshall,
I need your helicopter, hovercraft, and fire truck
to help deliver gifts to Adventure Bay."
"This pup's got to fly!" Skye exclaimed.
"Let's dive in!" Zuma cheered.
"I'm fired up!" Marshall declared.

"And, Chase," Ryder said, "I need your megaphone and net to help round up Santa's reindeer."

"Chase is on the case!" Chase shouted.

"All right! PAW Patrol is ready to roll!" Ryder
exclaimed, and all the pups raced away from
the Lookout.

Ryder, Rocky, and Rubble rode through the snowy night and found Santa's sleigh. Rubble got to work digging it out with the shovel in his Pup Pack. When he was finished, Rocky rolled his truck into position and lifted the sleigh.

Ryder inspected the damage.

"The crash broke off one of the runners," he said. "We'll have to replace it. Rocky, see what you have in your truck." The wind kicked up and snow spiraled through the air. "The storm is getting worse. We'd better get this fixed in a hurry."

While the sleigh was being repaired, Skye zoomed through the blustery night, looking for the lost bags of presents. Her searchlight scanned the dark forest below.

"I see a bag," she reported to Chase and Marshall. "Can you pups pick it up?"

Chase and Marshall skidded to a stop at the base of a tall tree. The bag was stuck in the high branches, so Marshall extended his truck's ladder. He carefully climbed to the top, but the bag was still too far away.

Marshall reached and stretched—and slipped off the ladder!

The bag tumbled down behind him.

Chase quickly launched a net to catch the falling bag of gifts. Marshall landed in the soft snow.
"I'm good," he announced with a smile.

Skye, Chase, and Marshall found the other bags of gifts and met Ryder at the sleigh. They got there just as Rocky started to attach an old ski to the bottom of the sleigh.

"I knew this would come in handy," he said proudly.

"Ryder, check out all the presents we found!"
Marshall shouted excitedly. "It's like Christmas!"
"It *is* Christmas, silly," Skye said with a chuckle.
Zuma arrived and brought his hovercraft to a
stop. "There are a lot of gifts to deliver. It's a good
thing they have names on them."

Ryder looked at the pups. "Skye, I need you and Marshall to drop gifts down chimneys. Zuma, you can deliver gifts to Seal Island. And, Chase, I need you to track down those reindeer."

"Yes, sir, Ryder, sir," Chase said.

The pups went to work.

Chase used his nose to follow some tracks in the snow. They led right to a reindeer.

"Bingo!" Chase exclaimed. "Wait, that's not a reindeer name. Come here, um, Blitzen?" The reindeer started to run away. "Donder? Cupid? Vixen? Prancer?"

At that, the reindeer stopped. "Santa needs to put tags on you guys," Chase said with a sigh.

Skye zoomed through the chilly air and swooped in over Katie's Pet Parlor. She dropped a gift down the chimney.

"Bull's-eye!" she exclaimed.

A few blocks away, Marshall tumbled down
Mayor Goodway's chimney and landed in her
living room with a thump.
"How does Santa do it?" he said to himself.
"*Bwok!*" said Chickaletta.

"*Shhh.* Don't wake the mayor," Marshall whispered as he put a present under the tree. Then he slid a gift-wrapped ear of corn over to the chicken.

"Merry Christmas, Chickaletta," he said, pushing his bag of gifts up the chimney.

Back at the sleigh, Rocky attached the old ski to the broken runner with a few quick twists of his screwdriver.

Ryder called Santa on his PupPad. "We've repaired your sleigh, and the pups are delivering the presents."

"You are all permanently on my Nice List!" Santa exclaimed. "But I still haven't found my Magic Christmas Star."

Rocky shook his head. "There will be a lot of disappointed boys and girls tomorrow."

"And pups," Rubble added.

"I have an idea!" Ryder announced.

Ryder replayed the Santa Tracker on his PupPad. "This should show us where the Magic Christmas Star fell."

"Looks like the star landed in Farmer Yumi's yard," said Rocky.

"Let's roll!" Ryder exclaimed, and he and the pups ran to their vehicles.

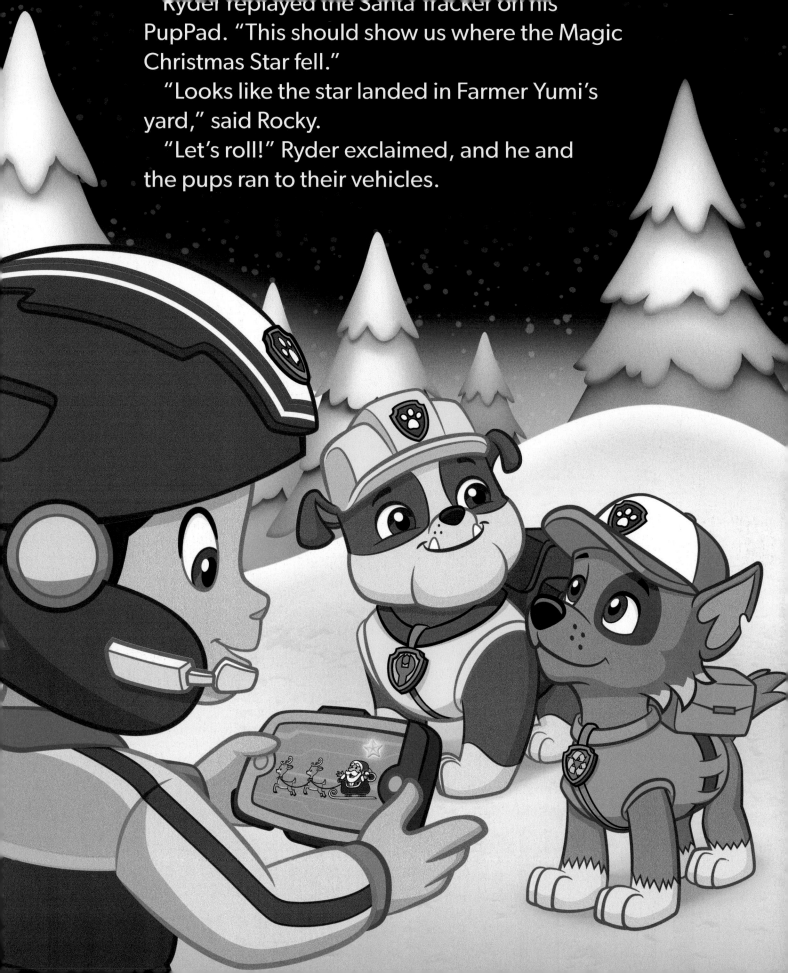

Meanwhile, out on the water, Zuma guided his hovercraft over the choppy waves. "I hope I make it to Cap'n Turbot's lighthouse before that storm comes back."

Wally the Walrus suddenly popped out of the water, blocking Zuma's way.

"Wally, I have to deliver these presents!" Zuma yelped.

Zuma tried to motor around Wally, but the big walrus kept getting in front of him and barking.

"Arf! Arf!"

Zuma realized he had a present for Wally. He dug through the bag of gifts and found a package shaped like a fish. He tossed it to Wally. "Merry Christmas, dude!"

Wally barked his thanks and moved so Zuma could speed away.

"It's got to be here somewhere," Ryder said
as he, Rocky, and Rubble searched outside
Farmer Yumi's barn for the Magic Christmas Star.
Rocky heard Bettina, Farmer Yumi's cow,
mooing. "Maybe Bettina saw it. Hey, where
is she?"
They glanced around, but no one saw her . . .
until Ryder pointed up at the night sky.

Ryder and the pups couldn't believe their
eyes. Bettina was flying through the air—
with the Christmas star stuck to her side!
"The star is making her fly like a reindeer!"
Ryder exclaimed.
"How will we get her down?" Rocky asked.

Ryder grabbed some hay and whistled to Bettina. "Fresh hay! Come and get it!"

Bettina floated down for her snack. While she was munching the hay, Rocky used a mechanical claw from his Pup Pack to grab the Magic Christmas Star.

"Good work!" Ryder cheered. He quickly called Santa to tell him the good news.

Meanwhile, Chase had found all eight of the reindeer, but they wouldn't line up. He decided this was a job for his loudspeaker.

"ATTENTION, ALL REINDEER!" he announced. "Please move forward in an orderly fashion!"

They did as they were told, and Chase led them back to Santa's sleigh.

When Ryder and the pups met at the sleigh,
they found Santa Claus waiting for them.
"My sleigh looks perfect!" he exclaimed.
"Except for one missing piece," Ryder said,
holding out the Magic Christmas Star. Santa took
it and hung it on the front of the sleigh.

While the pups loaded the gifts onto Santa's
sleigh, Skye playfully took hold of the reins and
pretended to be Santa. "I always wanted to sit
here! Now dash away, dash away, dash away,
all!"

The reindeer took off, pulling the sleigh—
and the pups!—through the air.

Santa laughed. "Ho, ho, ho! The reindeer
always go when they hear that!" He whistled,
and the reindeer landed back on the ground.

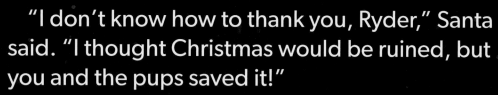

"I don't know how to thank you, Ryder," Santa said. "I thought Christmas would be ruined, but you and the pups saved it!"

"Whenever you're in trouble, just 'ho, ho, ho' for help!" Ryder replied as Santa climbed onto his sleigh and took to the sky.

Bright and early the next morning, the pups ran to their Christmas tree next to the Lookout. Santa had left gifts for everyone. But before the pups opened theirs, they wanted to give Ryder the present they had picked out just for him— a giant bone!

"It smells delicious," Chase said, licking his lips.

"It's perfect," Ryder said, laughing. "But I'll tell you what, pups—you can have it. Merry Christmas, everyone!"